I0831404

Charlotte Mary Yonge

Old Times at Otterbourne

Outlook

Charlotte Mary Yonge

Old Times at Otterbourne

1. Auflage | ISBN: 978-3-73261-937-5

Erscheinungsort: Paderborn, Deutschland

Erscheinungsjahr: 2018

Outlook Verlag GmbH, Paderborn.

Old Times at Otterbourne.

BY

CHARLOTTE M. YONGE.

[SECOND EDITION.]

Winchester:

WARREN AND SON, PRINTERS AND PUBLISHERS, HIGH STREET.

London:

SIMPKIN AND CO., LIMITED, STATIONERS' HALL COURT.

1891

Old Times at Otterbourne.

Not many of us remember Otterbourne before the Railroad, the Church, or the Penny Post. It may be pleasant to some of us to try to catch a few recollections before all those who can tell us anything about those times are quite gone.

To begin with the first that is known about it, or rather that is guessed. A part of a Roman road has been traced in Otterbourne Park, and near it was found a piece of a quern, one of the old stones of a hand mill, such as was used in ancient times for grinding corn; so that the place must have been inhabited at least seventeen hundred years ago. In the last century a medallion bearing the head of a Roman Emperor was found here, sixteen feet beneath the surface. It seems to be one of the medallions that were placed below the Eagle on the Roman Standards, and it is still in the possession of the family of Fitt, of Westley.

After the Roman and British times were over, this part of the country belonged to Wessex, the kingdom of the West Saxons, of which Winchester was the capital. Lying so near the chief town, which was the Bishop's throne, this place was likely soon to be made into a parish, when Archbishop Theodore divided England in dioceses and parishes, just twelve hundred years ago, for he died 690. The name no doubt means the village of the Otters, and even now these creatures are sometimes seen in the Itchen, so that no doubt there were once many more of them. The shapes and sizes of most of our parishes were fixed by those of the estates of the Lords who first built the Church for themselves and their households, with the churls and serfs on their manor. The first Lord of Otterbourne must have had a very long narrow property, to judge by the form of the parish, which is at least three miles long, and nowhere a mile in breadth. Most likely he wanted to secure as much of the river and meadow land as he could, with some high open heathy ground on the hill as common land where the cattle could graze, and some wood to supply timber and fuel. Probably all the slopes of the hills on each side of the valley of the Otter were covered with wood. The top of the gravelly hill to the southward was all heather and furze, as indeed it is still, and this reached all the way to Southampton and the Forest. The whole district was called Itene or Itchen, like the river. The name meant in the old English language, the Giant's Forest and the Giant's Wood.

The hill to the north was, as it still remains, chalk down. The village lay near the river and the stream that runs into it, upon the bed of clay between the chalk and the gravel. Most likely the Moathouse was then in existence, though a very different building from what it is at present, and its moat very deep and full of water, serving as a real defence. There is nothing left but broad hedge rows of the woods to the north-east, but one of these is called Dane Lane, and is said to be the road by which the Danes made their way to Winchester, being then a woodland path. It is said that whenever the yellow cow wheat grows freely the land has never been cultivated.

There was a hamlet at Boyatt, for both it and Otterbourne are mentioned in Domesday Book. This is the great census that William the Conqueror caused to be taken 1083 of all his kingdom. From it we learn that Otterbourne had a Church which belonged to Roger de Montgomery, a great Norman baron, whose father had been a friend of William I.

Well for the parish that it lay at a distance from the Giant's Wood, where the King turned out all the inhabitants for the sake of his "high deer," making it the New Forest. He and his sons could ride through down and heath all the way to their hunting. We all know how William Rufus was brought back from his last hunt, lying dead in the charcoal burner Purkis's cart, in which he was carried to his grave in Winchester Cathedral. Part of the road between Hursley and Otterbourne, near Silkstede, is called King's Lane, because it is said to have been the way by which this strange hearse travelled.

Silkstede is a farm now—it was most likely a grange, or outlying house belonging to some monastery—and there is a remnant of the gardens and some fine trees, and a hollow called China Dell, where snowdrops and double daffodils grow. But this is in Hursley parish, as is also Merdon Castle.

The green mounds and deep trenches, and the fragments of ruinous wall, have a story reaching far back into the ages.

There is little doubt, from their outline, that once there was an entrenched camp of the Romans on this ground, but nothing is known thereof. Merantune, as our Saxon ancestors called it, first is heard of when in 755 Cynewolf, King of Wessex, was murdered there by his kinsman Cyneheard, who was in his turn killed by the Thanes of the victim. With this savage story it first appears, but no more is known of its fate except that it became the property of the Bishops of Winchester, some say by the grant of Cynegyls, the first Christian King of Wessex, others by a later gift. It was then a manor, to which Hurstleigh, the woodland, was only an appendage; and the curious old manorial rights and customs plainly go back to these ancient præ-Norman times. To go through all the thirty customs would be impossible, but it is worth noting that the tenure of the lands descended by right to the youngest son in a family instead of the eldest. Such "cradle fiefs" exist in other parts of

England, and in Switzerland, on the principle that the elder ones go out into the world while their father is vigorous, but the youngest is the stay of his old age. The rents were at first paid in kind or in labour, with a heriot, namely, the most valuable animal in stock on a death, but these became latterly commuted for quit rent and fines. The trees were carefully guarded. Only one good timber tree on each holding in the life-time of a tenant might be cut by the Lord of the Manor, and the tenants themselves might only cut old rotten trees! But this is as much as you will wish to hear of these old customs, which prove that the Norman feudal system was kept out of this Episcopal manor. It was not even mentioned in Domesday Book, near as it was to Winchester. There it lay, peacefully on its island of chalk down, shut in by the well-preserved trees, till Stephen's brother, Bishop Henry de Blois, of Winchester, bethought him of turning the old Roman Camp into a fortified castle. The three Norman kings had wisely hindered the building of castles, but these sprung up like mushrooms under the feeble rule ofStephen.

The tenants must have toiled hard, judging by the massiveness of the small remnant, all built of the only material at hand, chalk to make mortar, in which flints are imbedded.

This fragment still standing used to be considered as part of the keep, but of late years better knowledge of the architecture of castles has led to the belief that it was part of the northern gateway tower. I borrow the description of the building from one written immediately after the comments of a gentleman who had studied the subject.

Henry de Blois, King Stephen's brother, Bishop of Winchester, probably wished for a stronghold near at hand, during his brother's wars with the Empress Maud. He would have begun by having the nearly circular embankment thrown up with a parapet along the top, and in the ditch thus formed a stockade of sharp pointed stakes. Within the court, the well, 300 feet deep, was dug, and round it would have been the buildings needed by the Bishop, his household and guards, much crowded together. The entrance would have been a drawbridge, across the great ditch, which on this side was not less than 60 feet wide and perhaps 25 deep, and through a great gateway between two high square towers which must have stood where now there is a slope leading down from the inner court, into the southern one. This slope is probably formed by the ruins of the gateway and tower being pitched into the ditch.

The Castle was then very small, and did not command the country except towards the south. The next work therefore would be to throw out an embankment to the south, with a ditch outside. The great gap whence Hursley House is seen, did not then exist, but there was an unbroken semicircle of rampart and ditch, which would protect a large number of men. In case of an enemy forcing this place, the defenders could retreat into the Castle by the drawbridge.

The entrance was on the eastern side, and in order to protect this and the back (or northern side) of the Castle, an embankment was thrown up outside the first moat, and with an outer moat of its own. Then, as, in case of this being carried by the enemy the defenders would be cut off from the main southern gateway, a square tower was built on this outer embankment exactly opposite to the ruin which yet remains, and only divided from it by the great ditch. On either side of the tower, cutting the embankment across therefore at right angles, was a little ditch spanned by a drawbridge, which, if the defenders found it necessary to retire to the tower, could at any time be raised. The foundations of the tower and the position of the ditch can still be distinctly traced.

Supposing farther that it became impossible to hold the tower, the besieged could retreat into the main body of the Castle by another drawbridge across the great ditch. This would lead them through the arch which can still be seen in the ruin, though it is partially blocked up. The room on the east side of this passage was probably a guard room.

These are all the remains. The embankments to the south and west command a great extent of country, and on the north and northwest, we trace the precautions by the great depth of the ditch, and steepness of the earthworks, though now overgrown with trees. All this must have been done between the years 1138 and 1154, and great part of the defences were thrown down in the lifetime of the founder. Merdon was not destined to shine in sieges, in spite of its strength. Henry II came in, and forbad the multiplication of castles and Merdon seems to have been dismantled as quickly as it had been built.

The Bishops of Winchester however still seem to have resided there from time to time, though it gradually fell into decay, and was ruinous by the end of the Plantagenet period.

After the younger Oliver's death, his sisters endeavoured to obtain the Hursley property to which their father had succeeded as his son's heir. He was past eighty and the judge allowed him to wear his hat at the trial in court, an act of consideration commended by Queen Anne.

After his death, in 1708, the estate was sold to the Heathcote family. The old house, whose foundations can be traced on the lawn, and which was approached by the two avenues of walnut trees still standing, was then pulled down, and the present one erected.

Most likely the oldest thing in Otterbourne is the arch that forms the doorway of the Boys' School, and which came from the door of the Old Church. By the carving on that arch, and the form of the little clustered columns that support it, we can tell that it must have been put up about the time of King Richard I or King John, somewhere about the year 1200. There was certainly a church before this date, but most likely this was the first time that much pains had been taken about its beauty, and carved stone had been brought from a distance. It was a good spot that was chosen, lying a little above the meadows, and not far from the moated Manor House. The east wall of the nave is still standing, but it now forms the west wall of the small remnant that is still covered in. It still has three arches in it, to lead to the old chancel, and above those arches there were some paintings. They came to light when the Old Church was pulled down. First, a great deal of plaster and whitewash came off. Then appeared part of the Commandments in Old English black letter, and below that, again, were some paintings, traced out in red upon the wall. They have been defaced so much that all that could be found out was that there was a quatrefoil shape within a square. The corners were filled up apparently with the emblems of the Four Cherubim, though only the Winged Ox showed plainly. There was a sitting figure in the centre, with the hand raised, and it was thought to be a very rude representation of our Blessed Lord in Judgment. In another compartment was an outline of a man, and another in a hairy garment, so that this last may have been intended for the Baptism of our Blessed Lord. Unfortunately, being on the outside wall, there was no means of protecting these curious paintings, and, sad to say, one evening, I myself saw a party of rough boys standing in a row throwing stones at them. There being a pathway through the churchyard, it was not possible to keep them out, and thus these curious remains have been destroyed.

We may think of the people who resorted to the little Old Church as wearing long gowns both men and women, on Sunday, spun, woven, and dyed blue at home, most likely with woad, a plant like mignonette which still grows in the lanes. The gentry were in gayer colours, but most likely none lived nearer than Winchester, and it was only when they plodded into market that the people would see the long-hanging sleeves, the pointed hoods, and the queer long-toed shoes of the young gentlemen, or the towers that the ladies put on their heads.

The name of Otterbourne does not come forward in history, but, as it lies so near Winchester, it must have had some share in what happened in the Cathedral city. The next thing we know about it is that Bishop Edyngton joined it to Hursley. William de Edyngton was Bishop of Winchester in the middle part of the reign of Edward III, from 1357 to 1366. Bishop de Pontissara founded a College at Winchester called St. Elizabeth's, and to assist in providing for the expenses, he decreed that the greater tithes of Hursley, those of the corn fields, should be paid to the Dean and Chapter, and that the rest of the tithe should go to the Vicar. Then, lest the Vicar should be too poor, Otterbourne was to be joined with Hursley, and held by the same parish priest, and this arrangement lasted for five hundred years. It was made in times when there was little heed taken to the real good of country places. The arrangement was confirmed by his successor, Bishop Edyngton, who lies buried in the nave of Winchester Cathedral, not far from where lies the much greater man who succeeded him. William of Wykeham went on with the work Edyngton had begun, and built the pillars of the Cathedral nave as we now see them. He also founded the two Colleges of St. Mary, one at Winchester for 70 boys, one at Oxford to receive the scholars as they grew older, meaning that they should be trained up to become priests. It seems that the old name of the field where the college stands was Otterbourne meadow, and that it was bought of a Master Dummer. Bishop Wykeham's College at Oxford is still called New College, though there are now many much newer. One small estate at Otterbourne was given by him to help to endow Winchester College, to which it still belongs.

Good men had come to think that founding colleges was the very best thing they could do for the benefit of the Church, and William of Waynflete, who was made Bishop of Winchester in 1447, founded another college at Oxford in honour of St. Mary Magdalen. To this College he gave large estates for its maintenance, and in especial a very large portion of our long, narrow parish of Otterbourne. Ever since his time, two of the Fellows of Magdalen, if not the President himself, have come with the Steward, on a progress through the estates every year to hold their Court and give audit to all who hold lands of them Till quite recently the Court was always held at the Manor House, the old Moat House, which must once have been the principal house in the parish, though now it is so much gone to decay. Old Dr. Plank, the President of Magdalen, used to come thither in Farmer Colson's time. What used to be the principal room has a short staircase leading to it, and in the wainscot over the fire-place is a curious old picture, painted, I fancy, between 1600 and 1700, showing a fight between turbaned men and European soldiers, most likely Turks and Austrians. It is a pity that it cannot tell its history. The moat goes all round the house, garden, and farmyard, and no doubt used to have a drawbridge. Forty or fifty years ago, it was clear and had fish in it, but the bridge fell in and choked the stream, and since that it has become full of reeds and a mere swamp. It must have been a really useful protection in the evil times of the Wars of the Roses.

Most likely the Commandments were painted over the old fresco on the east wall of the nave of the old Church either in the time of Edward VI, or Elizabeth, for if they had been later, the letters would not have been Old English. The foreigners who meddled so much with our Church in the latter years of Edward VI obtained that the Holy Communion should not be celebrated in the chancels, but that the Holy Table should be spread in the body of the Church, and many Chancels were thus disused and became ruinous, as ours most certainly did at some time or other. St. Elizabeth's College was broken up and the place where it stood given to the college of St. Mary. It is still called Elizabeth Meadow. The presentation to the Cure of our two parishes went with the estate of Hursley.

There was a very odd scene somewhere between Winchester and Southampton in the year 1554. Queen Mary Tudor was waiting at Winchester for her bridegroom, Philip of Spain. He landed at Southampton on the morning of the 20th of July, and set out in a black velvet dress, red cloak, and black velvet hat, with a splendid train of gentlemen to ride to Winchester. It was a very wet day, and the Queen sent a gentleman with a ring from her, to beg him to come no farther in the rain. But the gentleman knew no Spanish, and the King no English. So Philip thought some warning of treachery was meant, and halted in great doubt and difficulty till the messenger recollected his French, and said in that tongue, that the Queen was only afraid of his Grace's getting wet. So on went Philip, and the High Sheriff of Hampshire rode before him with a long white wand in his hand, and his hat off, the rain running in streams off his bare head. They went so slowly as not to reach Winchester till six or seven o'clock in the evening, so that the people of Otterbourne, Compton, and Twyford must have had a good view of the Spanish Prince who was so unwelcome to them all.

Thomas Sternhold, who together with Hopkins put the Psalms into metre for singing, lived in the outskirts of Hursley.

When the plunder of the Monasteries was exhausted, the Tudor Sovereigns, or perhaps their favourites, took themselves to exacting gifts and grants from the Bishops, and thus Poynet who was intended in the stead of Gardiner gave Merdon to Edward VI, who presented it to Sir Philip Hobby. It was recovered by Bishop Gardiner, but granted back again by Queen Elizabeth. Sir Philip is believed to have first built a mansion at Hursley, and his nephew sold the place to Sir Thomas Clarke, who was apparently a hard lord of the manor. His tenants still had to labour at his crops instead of paying rent, but provisions had to be found them. About the year 1600, on the arrival of a hogshead of porridge, unsavoury and full of worms, the reapers struck, and their part was taken by Mr. Robert Coram, who then owned Cranbury, so hotly that he and Mr. Pye, Sir Thomas Clarke's steward, rode at one another through the wheat with drawn daggers. Lady Clarke yielded, and cooked two or three bacon-hogs for the reapers.

The old road from Winchester to Southampton then went along what we now call the Old Hollow, leading from Shawford Down to Oakwood. Then it seems to have gone along towards the old Church, its course being still marked by the long narrow meadows, called the Jar Mead and Hundred Acres, or, more properly, Under an Acre. Then it led down to the ford at Brambridge, for there was then no canal to be crossed. The only great personage who was likely to have come along this road in the early 17th century was King James the First's wife, Queen Anne of Denmark, who spent a winter at the old Castle of Winchester, and was dreadfully dull there, though the ladies tried to amuse her by all sorts of games, among which one was called "Rise, Pig, and Go."

James I gave us one of the best of Bishops, Lancelot Andrewes by name, who wrote a beautiful book of devotions. He lived on to the time of Charles I, and did much to get the ruins made in the bad days round Winchester Cathedral cleared and set to rights. Most likely he saw that the orders for putting the altars back into their right places were carried out, and very likely the chancel was then mended, but with no attention to architecture, for the head of the east window was built up anyhow with broken bits of tracery from a larger and handsomer one. The heir of the Clarkes sold the property at Hursley to Mr. Mayor, to whose only daughter Oliver Cromwell married his son Richard.

What happened here in the Great Rebellion we do not know. An iron ball was once dug up in the grounds at Otterbourne House, which may have come from Oliver's Battery; but it is also said to be only the knob of an old pump handle—

"When from the guarded down
Fierce Cromwell's rebel soldiery kept watch o'er Wykeham's town.
They spoiled the tombs of valiant men, warrior, and saint, and sage;
But at the tomb of Wykeham good angels quenched their rage."

Colonel Nathanael Fiennes prevented harm from being done to the College or the monuments in the Cathedral; but there was some talk of destroying that holy place, for I have seen a petition from the citizens of Winchester that it might be spared. It is said that some loyal person took out all the stained glass in the great west window, hid it in a chest, and buried it; but when better times came, it could not be restored to what it was before, and was put in confusedly, as we now see it.

Stoneham had a brave old clergyman, who kept possession of his church and rectory all through the war, and went on with the service till he died, no man daring to meddle with him. But Otterbourne was sure to follow the fate of Hursley. The King's Head Inn at Hursley is thought to have been so called in allusion to the death of King Charles I. A strange compliment to the Cromwells.

Richard had a large family, most of whom died young, as may be seen on their monument in Hursley Church. It was at this time that the customs of the Manor were put on record in writing. The son, Oliver, lived till 1705, and was confounded in the country people's minds with his grandfather.

There is an odd, wild story, that Cromwell sunk all his treasure in the great well at Merdon Castle, in Hursley Park, 300 feet deep. It was further said, if it were drawn up again, that no one must speak till it was safe, otherwise it would be lost. A great chest was raised to the mouth of the well, when one of the men said, "Here it comes!" The rope broke, it fell back, and no one ever saw it more. Most likely this is an old legend belonging to the Castle long before, and only connected with Oliver Cromwell because he was an historical person. Certain it is that when the well was cleared out about 30 or 40 years ago nothing was found but two curious old candlesticks, and a great number of pins, which had been thrown down because they caused those curious reverberations in the great depth. Another legend is that Merdon Well is connected with the beautiful clear spring at Otterbourne called Pole Hole or Pool Hole, so that when a couple of ducks were thrown down the well, they came out at Pole Hole with all their feathers scraped off.

It was in the time of the Commonwealth, in 1653, that our first parish register begins. Some parishes have much older ones, so, perhaps, ours may have been destroyed. The first entry in this old parchment book is that Elizabeth, daughter of Edward Cox, of Otterbourne, and Anne, his wife, was born –. A large stain has made the rest of this entry illegible. There are only three births in 1653, and seven in 1654, one of these William, son of Mr. William Downe, of Otterbourne Farm, and Joane, his wife, is, however, marked with two black lines beneath the entry, as are his sisters, Elizabeth and Jane, 1656 and 1658, apparently to do honour to the principal inhabitant.

It is to be observed that all the entries here are of births, not of baptisms, departing from the general rule of Church registers, and they are all in English; but in 1663 each child is recorded as baptized, and the Latin language is used. This looks much as if a regular clergyman, a scholar, too, had, after the Restoration, become curate of the parish. He does not sign his registers, so we do not know his name. In 1653 the banns of William Downe and Jane Newman were published September 17th and the two Lord's Days ensuing, but their wedding is not entered, and the first marriage recorded is that of Matthew Dummer and Jane Burt, in 1663. The first funeral was Emelin, wife of Robert Purser, in 1653.

Also, there was plenty of brick-making, for King Charles II had planned to build a grand palace at Winchester on the model of the great French palace of Versailles, and it is said that Dell copse was formed by the digging out of bricks for the purpose. It was to reach all over the downs, with fountains and water playing in them, and a great tower on Oliver's Battery, with a light to guide the ships in the Channel. There is a story that Charles, who was a capital walker, sometimes walked over from Southampton to look at his buildings. One of the gentlemen who attended him let the people at Twyford know who was going that way. So they all turned out to look at him, which was what the King by no means wished. So he avoided them, and punished his indiscreet courtier by taking a run and crossing one of the broad streams with a flying leap, then proceeding on to Winchester, leaving his attendant to follow as best he might.

After all only one wing of the intended palace was built. For a long time it was called the King's House, but now it is only known as the Barracks. The work must have led to an increase in the population, for more baptisms are recorded in the register, though not more than six or seven in each year, all carefully set down in Latin, though with no officiating minister named. There is an Augustine Thomas, who seems to have had a large family, and who probably was the owner of the ground on which the vicarage now stands, the name of which used to be Thomas's Bargain.

There must have been a great quickening of activity in Otterbourne soon after the Restoration, for it was then that the Itchen canal or barge river, as it used to be called, was dug, to convey coals from Southampton, and, of course, this much improved the irrigation of the water meadows. This canal was one of the first made in England, and was very valuable for nearly two hundred years, until the time of railways.

In 1690, a larger parchment register was provided, and every two years it appears to have been shown up to the magistrates at the Petty Sessions, and signed by two of them.

At this time there seem to have been some repairs of the church. Certainly, a great square board painted with the royal arms was then erected, for it bore the date 1698, and the initials "W. M." for William and Mary. There it was, on a beam, above the chancel arch, and the lion and unicorn on either side, the first with a huge tongue hanging out at the corner of his mouth, looking very complacent, as though he were displaying the royal arms, the unicorn slim and dapper with a chain hanging from his neck.

Several of our old surnames appear about this time, Cox, Comley, Collins, Goodchild, Woods, Wareham. John Newcombe, Rector of Otterbourne, who afterwards became Bishop of Llandaff, signs his register carefully, but drops the Latin, as various names may be mentioned, Scientia, or Science Olden, Philadelphia Comley, and Dennis Winter, who married William Westgate. Anne and Abraham were the twin children of John and Anne Didimus, in 1741.

The first church rate book only begins in 1776, but it is curious as showing to whom the land then belonged. The spelling is also odd, and as the handwriting is beautiful, so there is no doubt that it really is an account of the Church *Raiting*, nor that the "rait" was "mead." Walter Smythe, Esquire, of Brambridge, appears, also John Colson John Comley, and Charles Vine. Lincolns belonged to Mr. Kentish and Gun Plot to Thilman.

The expenditure begins thus:—April 9, 1776, "Pd. Short for 6 dozen sparw heds," and the sparw heds are repeated all down the page, varied with what would shock the H. H.—3*d.* for foxheads. Also "expenses ad visitation" 9*s.* 6*d.*, and at the bottom of the page, the parish is thus mentioned as creditor "out of pockets, 5*s.* 1*d.*" In 1777 however, though the vestry paid "Didums 1 badger's head, 1 polecat's head; Hary Bell for 2 marten cats, and spares innumerable, and the clarck warges, £1. 5*s.*, there was £1. 3*s.* in hand." The polecats and marten cats were soon exterminated, but foxes, hedgehogs, and sparrows continue to appear, though in improved spelling, till April 24th, 1832, when this entry appears:—"At a meeting called to elect new Churchwardens, present the Rev. R. Shuckburgh, curate, and only one other person present, the meeting is adjourned. Mr. Shuckburgh protests most strongly against the disgraceful custom of appropriating money collected for Church rates towards destroying vermin on the farms." And this put an end to the custom. However, there were more rightful expenses. Before Easter there is paid "for washan the surples" 4*s.* It would seem that the Holy Communion was celebrated four times a year, and that the Elements were paid for every time at 3*s.* 7*d.* In 1784, when there was a great improvement in spelling, there were some repairs done—"Paid for Communion cloth, 10 pence, and for washing and marking it, 6p." In 1786 there was a new church bell, costing £5. 5*s.* 10*d.* Aaron Chalk, whom some of the elder inhabitants may remember, a very feeble old man walking with two sticks, was in that year one of the foremost traders in sparrow heads. It gives a curious sense of the lapse of time to think of those tottering limbs active in bird catching.

May 2, in 1783, we find the entry "paid for the caraidge of the old bell and the new one downe from London, 11*s.* 10*d.* May 22—Paid William Branding bill for hanging the new bell, £1. 13*s.*" Altogether, at the end of the year, it is recorded "the book in debt" £1. 11*s.*, but "the disburstments," as they are spelt, righted themselves in 1784, when we find "paid for musick for the use of the Church, £1. 1*s.* To George Neal for whitewashing Church, £1. 1*s.*, George Neale, two days' work, 5*s.* 3*d.*, for work in the gallery, 19*s.* 4*d.*, bill for tiles, 3*s.* 4*d.*"

The only connection Otterbourne has with any historical person is not a pleasant one. The family of Smythe, Roman Catholics, long held Brambridge, and they endowed a little Roman Catholic Chapel at Highbridge. At one time, a number of their tenants and servants were of the same communion, and there is a note in the parish register by the curate to say that there were several families at Allbrook and Highbridge whose children he had not christened, though he believed they had been baptized by the Roman Catholic priest. One of the daughters of the Smythe family was the beautiful Mrs. Fitz-Herbert, whom the Prince of Wales, afterwards George IV, was well known to have privately married. He never openly avowed this, because by the law made in the time of William III, a marriage with a Roman Catholic disqualifies for the succession to the crown; besides which, under George III, members of the royal family had been prohibited from marrying without the King's consent, and such marriages were declared null and void. The story is mentioned here because an idea has gone abroad that the wedding took place in the chapel at Highbridge, but this is quite untrue. The ceremony was performed at Brighton, and it is curious that the story of it having happened here only began to get afloat after the death of Mr. Newton, the last of the old servants who had known Mrs. Fitz-Herbert. Walter Smythe, her brother, was one of the *détenus* whom Napoleon I kept prisoners, though only English travellers, on the rupture of the Peace of Amiens. His brother, Charles, while taking care of the estate, had all the lime trees in the avenue pollarded, and sold the tops to make stocks for muskets.

In those days there was only a foot bridge across the Itchen at Brambridge. Carts and carriages had to ford the river, not straight across, but making a slight curve downwards; this led to awkward accidents. There was a gentleman dining with Mr. Walter Smythe, who was pressed to sleep at Brambridge, but declined, saying that he liked to have all his little comforts about him. When daylight came, the poor man was found seated on the top of his chaise, the water flowing through the windows below; for the post boy had taken a wrong turn, and, being afraid to move, had been forced to remain in the river till the morning. A far worse disaster befel the Newton family on their way to a funeral. It is described by one of the bearers: "When the cart turned over, the corpse was on the foot bridge. It was a very wet day, and the wind was blowing furiously at the time. It had a great effect on the cart, as it was a narrow cart with a tilt on, and there was a long wood sill at the side of the river. That dropping of the sill caused the accident. I think there were five females in the cart and the driver. The water was as much as 4ft. deep and running very sharp, so myself and others went into the water to fetch them out, and when we got to the cart they were all on the top of the other, with their heads just out of the water. They could not go on to church with the corpse, and we had a very hard job to save the horse from being drowned, as his head was but just out of the water."

All through the time of the long war with France there was here, as well as everywhere else around the coast, fear of a landing of the French. The flat-bottomed boats to bring the French over were actually ready at Boulogne, and the troops mustered to come across in them. On our side, volunteers were in training in case of need, and preparations were made for sending off the women and children inland on the first news of the enemy landing. Not very many years ago there were still to be seen in a barn at Hursley the planks prepared to fit as seats into the waggons that were to carry them away. And a family living here are said to have kept everything packed up, even the fireirons, and to have stirred up the fire with a stick during a whole winter. However, by God's blessing and our fleets and armies, the danger was kept from our doors.

With the activity that followed upon the peace came a great deal of road-making. The present high road between Winchester and Southampton was then made, and the way cut through the hills—Otterbourne Hill and Compton Hill on either side. This led to the main part of the inhabitants settling in the village street, instead of round the old Church as before. Another great road was made at the same time—that which crosses Golden Common and leads ultimately to Portsmouth. It used to be called Cobbett's Road, because William Cobbett, a clever, self-taught man, had much to do with laying it out. Cobbett had a good many theories which he tried to put into practice, some sensible, others mistaken. The principal traces we see of him now are in the trees that he planted, chiefly introduced from America. He thought the robinia, or false acacia, would make good hedges, because of its long thorns and power of throwing up suckers, and many people planted them, but they proved too brittle to be of much use, though some are still growing. He was a friend of Mr. Harley, who then owned Otterbourne House, and planted many curious trees there, of which two long remained—a hickory nut and a large tree in the drive. There was also an oak with enormous leaves, but it was planted so near the house that it had to be moved, and died in consequence.

These roads were for the coaches. Young folks, who never saw anything nearer approaching to a stage coach than the drags some gentlemen keep, can hardly fancy what these stage coaches were—tall vehicles, holding four inside passengers and at least twelve outside and quantities of luggage. They were drawn by four of the strongest and quickest horses that could be procured, and these were changed about every five or six miles, so as to keep up full speed. The coachman, generally a big, burly man, with a face reddened by exposure to the weather, and often by a glass of ale at every stage, sat on the box in a drab coat, with many capes one over the other. The seat next to him was the favourite one with the passengers, and gentlemen would sometimes bribe coachmen to let them drive; nay, some gentlemen actually took to the trade themselves. There was also a guard, who in mail coaches took care of the post bags, and dropped them at the places where they were intended for. In the days when highwaymen infested the roads the guard had carried pistols, and still the guard of the mail wore a red coat, and blew a horn on entering any place to warn the people to bring out their post bags and exchange them for others.

One or two coaches kept their horses at the White Horse, so as to be fresh for going up the hill, others at the Cricketers, while others changed at Compton and the New Hut. Some of the stables still remain, converted into cottages. The horses were fine animals, beautifully kept; but the habit of hanging about public-houses to attend to them was not good for the ostlers and people concerned. About fifteen coaches came through this place in the morning, and their fellows in the evening, each proprietor keeping two coaches, starting from the two opposite ends at the same time. There was the Mail, the Telegraph, the Independent, the Red Rover, the Hirondelle, all London coaches, besides the Oxford coach and some that only ran between Winchester and Southampton. The driver and owner of one, Mason's coach, was only a few years ago living here. When people intended to go on a journey, they booked their places a day or two beforehand, but for short journeys or going into Winchester they would watch for a vacant space in a coach as it passed by.

It is odd to look back at an old article in a quarterly review describing coach travelling as something so swift and complete that it could not be surpassed in its perfection. Yet accidents with the spirited horses and rapid driving were not uncommon, and a fall from an overloaded coach was a dangerous thing.

When the mail went by coach the sending of letters and parcels could not but be expensive. Heavy goods travelled by waggon, barge, or ship, parcels went by carriers or by coaches, and nothing could be posted but what was quite light. So postage was very expensive, and it is strange to look back on the regulations connected with it. Our readers under forty years old will hardly believe the rates that were paid for postage, varying according to distance. There was a company in London that carried letters from one part of that town to another for twopence apiece, and this was the cheapest post in England. A letter from London to Otterbourne cost eightpence, and one from Winchester either threepence or fourpence, one from Devonshire elevenpence, and this was paid not by the sender, but by the receiver. It was reckoned impolite to prepay a letter. Moreover, the letter had to be on a single sheet. The sheet might be of any size that could be had, but it must be only one. Asmall sheet enclosed within another, or the lightest thing, such as a lock of hair or a feather, made it a double letter, for which double postage had to be given. The usual custom was to write on quarto sheets twice the size of what is used now, and, after filling three sides, to fold the fourth, leaving a space for the direction and the seal, and then to write on the flaps and in the space over "My dear –," sometimes crossing the writing till the whole letter was chequer work. For if the letter was to cost the receiver so much, it seemed fair to let him get as much as possible. Letters were almost always sealed, and it took neat and practised hands to fold and seal them nicely, without awkward corners sticking out.

Newspapers, if folded so as to show the red Government stamp, went for a penny, but nothing might be put into them, and not a word beyond the address written on them. The reason of all this was that the cost of carriage was then so great that it could only be made to answer by those high rates, and by preventing everything but real letters and newspapers from being thus taken. As Government then, as now, was at the expense of postage, its own correspondence went free, and therefore all Members of Parliament had the privilege of sending letters freely. They were allowed to post eleven a day, which might contain as much as would weigh an ounce, without charge, if they wrote the date at the top and their name in the right hand corner. This was called franking, and plenty of letters by no means on public business travelled in that way.

There was no post office in Otterbourne till between 1836 and 1840; for, of course there were few letters written or received, and thus it did not seem to many persons worth while for village children to learn to write. If they did go into service at a distance from home, their letters would cost more than their friends could afford to pay. This was a sad thing, and broke up and cut up families very much more than any distance does now. It really is easier to keep up intercourse with a person in America or even New Zealand now, than it was then with one in Scotland, Northumberland, or Cornwall; for travelling was so expensive that visits could seldom be made, and servants could not go to their homes unless they were within such a short distance as to be able to travel by coach or by carrier's cart, or even walking all the way, getting a cast now and then by a cart.

People who did not travel by coaches, or who went where there was no coach, hired post-chaises, close carriages something like flies. Most inns, where the coaches kept their horses, possessed a post-chaise, and were licensed to let out post horses for hire. Most of the gentlefolks' families kept a close carriage called a chariot, and, if they did not keep horses of their own, took a pair of post-horses, one of which was ridden by a man, who, whatever might be his age, was always called a post-boy. Some inns dressed their post-boys in light blue jackets, some in yellow ones, according to their politics, but the shape was always the same; corduroy tights, top boots, and generally white (or rather drab-coloured) hats. It used to be an amusement to watch whether the post-boy would be a blue or a yellow one at each fresh stage. Hardly any one knows what a post-boy was like now, far less an old-fashioned travelling carriage or chariot and its boxes.

The travelling carriage was generally yellow. It had two good seats inside, and a double one had a second seat, where two persons sat backwards. The cushion behind lifted up and disclosed a long narrow recess called the swordcase, because, when there were highwaymen on the roads, people kept their weapons there. There were sometimes two, sometimes one seat outside, called the box and the dickey—much the pleasantest places, for it was very easy to feel sick and giddy inside. A curved splashboard went up from the bottom of the chariot to a level with the window, and within it fitted what was called the cap box, with a curved bottom, so that when in a house it had to be set down in a frame to hold it upright. A big flat box, called the imperial, in which ladies put their dresses, was on the top of the carriage, two more long, narrow ones, generally used for shoes and linen, fitted under the seat, and another square one was hung below the dickey at the back, and called the drop box. Such a mischance has been known as, on an arrival, a servant coming in with the remains of this black box between his arms, saying—"Sir, should not this box have a bottom to it?" The chariot thus carried plenty of goods, and was a sort of family home on a journey. To go to Plymouth, which now can be done in six or seven hours, then occupied two long days, halting for the night to sleep at an inn.

The Old Church

Some of us can still remember the old Church and the old Sunday habits prevailing before 1830. The Churchyard was large and very pretty, though ill kept, surrounded with a very open railing, and with the banks sloping towards the water meadows clothed with fine elm trees—one with a large and curious excrescence on the bark. There was a deep porch on the south side of the Church, with seats on each side. Then, on red tiles, one entered between two blocks of pews of old brown unpainted oak (their doors are panels to the roof of the boys' school). In the space between them were two or three low benches for the children. There were three arches leading to the chancel, but that on the south side was closed by the pulpit and reading desk, and that on the north by a square pew belonging to Cranbury. Within the chancel on the north side was a large pew lined with red, belonging to Cranbury, and on the south, first the clerk's desk, then a narrow seat of the clergyman's, and then a large square pew. Boys in the morning and men in the afternoon used to sit on the benches placed outside these, and beyond was the rail shutting in the Altar, which was covered with red cloth, and stood below a large window, on each side of which were the Commandments in yellow letters on a blue ground, and on the wall were painted the two texts, "The Cup of Blessing, is it not the Communion of the Blood of Christ?" and "The Bread which we break, is it not the Communion of the Body of Christ?" The vestry was built out to the north, and was entered from the sanctuary.

Further space was provided by two galleries, one on the north side, supported on iron poles, and entered from the outside by a step ladder studded with large square-headed nails to prevent it from being slippery. The other went across the west end, and was entered by a dark staircase leading up behind the pews, which further led to the little square weather-boarded tower containing two beautifully toned bells. These were rung from the outer gallery where the men sat. There was a part boarded off for the singers. The Font was nearly under the gallery. It was of white marble, and still lines our present Font. Tradition says it was given by a former clerk, perhaps Mr. Fidler, but there is no record of it. An older and much ruder Font was hidden away under the gallery stairs close to an old chest, where women sometimes found a seat, against the west wall.

In those days, now more than half a century ago, when Archdeacon Heathcote was Vicar, he or his Curate used to ride over from Hursley on Sunday for the service at Otterbourne. There was only one service, alternately in the morning and afternoon, at half-past ten or at three, or in the winter at half-past two. The time was not much fixed, for on a new comer asking when the service would take place, the answer was "at half-past two, sir, or at three, or else no time at all," by which was meant no exact hour or half-hour. This uncertainty led to the bells never being rung till the minister was seen turning the corner of Kiln-lane, just where the large boulder stone used to be. The congregation was, however, collecting, almost all the men in white smocks with beautifully worked breasts and backs, the more well-to-do in velveteen; the women in huge bonnets. The elder ones wore black silk or satin bonnets, with high crowns and big fronts, the younger ones, straw with ribbon crossed over, always with a bonnet cap under. A red cloak was the regular old women's dress, or a black or blue one, and sometimes a square shawl, folded so as to make a triangle, over a gown of stuff in winter, print in summer. A blue printed cotton with white or yellow sprays was the regular week day dress, and the poorest wore it on Sundays. The little girls in the aisle had the like big coarse straw bonnets, with a strip of glazed calico hemmed and crossed over for strings, round tippets, and straight print frocks down to their feet. The boys were in small smocks, of either white or green canvas, with fustian or corduroy jackets or trowsers below, never cloth. Gloves and pocket handkerchiefs were hardly known among the children, hardly an umbrella, far less parasols or muffs. Ladies had pelisses for out-of-door wear, fitting close like ulsters, but made of dark green or purple silk or merino, and white worked dresses under them in summer.

Well, the congregation got into Church—three families by the step ladder to one gallery, and the men into another, where the front row squeezed their knees through the rails and leant on the top bar, the rest of the world in the pews, and the children on benches. The clerk was in his desk behind the reading desk—good George Oxford, with his calm, good, gentle face, and tall figure, sadly lame from rheumatism caught when working in the brick kilns. His voice was always heard above the others in the responses, but our congregation never had dropped the habit of responding, and, though there was no chanting, the Amens and some of the Versicles used to have a grand full musical sound peculiar to that Church. People also all turned to the east for the Creed, few knelt, but some of the elder men stood during the prayers, and, though there was far too much *sitting down* during the singing, every body got up and stood, if "Hallelujah" occurred, as it often did in anthems.

There were eight or ten singers, and they had a bassoon, a flute, and a clarionet. They used to sing before the Communion Service in the morning, after the Second Lesson in the afternoon, and before each Sermon. Master Oxford had a good voice, and was wanted in the choir, so as soon as the General Thanksgiving began, he started off from his seat, and might be heard going the length of the nave, climbing the stairs, and crossing the outer gallery. Sometimes he took his long stick with him, and gave a good stripe across the straw bonnet of any particularly naughty child. In the gallery he proclaimed—"Let us sing to the praise and glory of God in the Psalm," then giving the first line.

The Psalms were always from the New or Old Versions. A slate with the number in chalk was also hung out—23 O.V., 112 N.V., as the case might be. About four verses of each were sung, the last lines over and over again, some very oddly divided. For instance—

> "Shall fix the place where we must dwell,
> The pride of Jacob, His delight,"

was sung thus:—

> "The pride of Ja—the pride of Ja—the pride of Ja—" (at least three times before the line was ended).

But rough as these were, some of these Psalms were very dear to us all, specially the old twenty-third:—

> "My Shepherd is the living Lord,
>   Nothing, therefore, I need,
> In pastures fair, by pleasant streams
>   He setteth me to feed.
>
> He shall convert and glad my soul,
>   And bring my soul in frame
> To walk in paths of holiness,
>   For His most Holy Name.
>
> I pass the gloomy vale of death,
>   From fear and danger free;
> For there His guiding rod and staff
>   Defend and comfort me."

Another much-loved one was the 121st:—

> "To Zion's hill I lift my eyes,
>   From thence expecting aid,
> From Zion's hill and Zion's God,
>   Who heaven and earth hath made.
>
> Sheltered beneath the Almighty's wings,

Thou shall securely rest,
Where neither sun nor moon shall thee
By day nor night molest.

Then thou, my soul, in safety rest,
Thy Guardian will not sleep,
His watchful care, that Israel guards,
Shall Israel's monarch keep.

At home, abroad, in peace or war,
Thy God shall thee defend,
Conduct thee through life's pilgrimage,
Safe to thy journey's end."

Will the sight of these lines bring back to any one the old tune, the old sounds, the old sights of the whitewashed Church, and old John Green in the gallery, singing with his bass voice, with all his might, his eyebrows moving as he sung? And then the Commandments and Ante-Communion read not from the Altar, but the desk; the surplice taken off in the desk instead of the Vestry; Master Oxford's announcements shouted out from his place, generally after the Second Lesson—"I hereby give notice that a Vestry Meeting will be held on Tuesday, at twelve o'clock, to make a new rate for the relief of the poo-oor." "I hereby give notice that Evening Service will be at half-past two as long as the winter days are short." Well, we should think these things odd now, and we have much to be thankful for in the changes; but there were holy and faithful ones then, and Master Oxford was one of them.

In the days here described, from 1820 to 1827, few small villages had anything but dame schools, and Otterbourne children, such as had any schooling at all, were sent to Mrs. Yates's school on the hill, where she sat, the very picture of the old-fashioned mistress, in her black silk bonnet, with the children on benches before her, and her rod at hand.

Several families, however, did not send the children to school at all, and there were many who could not read, many more who could not write, and there was very little religious teaching, except that in the Sunday afternoons in Lent, the catechism was said in Church by the best instructed children, but without any explanation.

About the year 1819 Mrs. Bargus and her daughter came to live at Otterbourne, and in 1822 Miss Bargus married William Crawley Yonge, who had retired from the army, after serving in the Peninsula and at Waterloo. Both Mr. and Mrs. Yonge had clergymen for their fathers, and were used to think much of the welfare of their neighbours. It was not, however, till 1823 that Mrs. Yonge saw her way to beginning a little Sunday School for girls, teaching it all by herself, in a room by what is now Mr. J. Misselbrook's house. While there was still only one Service on Sundays, she kept the school on the vacant half of the day, reading the Psalms and Lessons to the children, who were mostly biggish girls. This was when Archdeacon Heathcote was the Vicar of Hursley and Otterbourne, and the Rev. Robert Shuckburgh was his Curate. Archdeacon and Mrs. Heathcote, who were most kind and liberal, gave every help and assisted in setting up the Clothing Club.

Mrs. Yonge's first list of Easter prizes contains twenty names of girls, and the years that have passed have left but few of them here. A large Bible bound in plain brown leather was the highest prize; Prayer Books, equally unornamented, New Testaments, and Psalters, being books containing only the Psalms and Matins and Evensong, were also given, and were then, perhaps, more highly valued than the dainty little coloured books every one now likes to have for Sunday. Then there were frocks, coarse straw bonnets, and sometimes pocket handkerchiefs, for these were not by any means such universal possessions as could be wished, and only came out on Sunday. As to gloves, silk handkerchiefs, parasols, muffs, or even umbrellas, the children thought them as much out of their reach as a set of pearls or diamonds, but what was worse, their outer clothing was very insufficent, seldom more than a thin cotton frock and tippet, and the grey duffle cloaks, which were thought a great possession, were both slight and scanty.

About 1826, Mrs. Yonge was looking at the bit of waste land that had once served as a roadway to the field at the back of Otterbourne House, when she said, "How I wish I had money enough to build a school here." "Well," said Mrs. Bargus, "You shall have what I can give." The amount was small, but with it Mr. Yonge contrived to put up one room with two new small ones at the back, built of mud rough cast, and with a brick floor, except for the little bedroom being raised a step, and boarded.

The schoolroom was intended to hold all the children who did not go to Mrs. Yates, both boys and girls, and it was sufficient, for, in the first place, nobody from Fryern-hill came. Mrs. Green had a separate little school there. Then the age for going to school was supposed to be six. If anyone sent a child younger, the fee was threepence instead of a penny. The fee for learning writing and arithmetic was threepence, for there was a general opinion that they were of little real use, and that writing letters would waste time (as it sometimes certainly does). Besides this, the eldest daughter of a family was always minding the baby, and never went to school; and boys were put to do what their mothers called "keeping a few birds" when very small indeed, while other families were too rough to care about education so that the numbers were seldom over thirty.

There were no such people as trained mistresses then. The National Society had a school for masters, but they were expensive and could only be employed in large towns; so all that could be looked for was a kind, motherly, good person who could read and do needlework well. And the first mistress was Mrs. Creswick, a pleasant-looking person with a pale face and dark eyes, who had been a servant at Archdeacon Heathcote's, and had since had great troubles. She did teach the Catechism, reading, and work when the children were tolerably good and obeyed her, but boys were a great deal too much for her, and she had frail health, and such a bad leg that she never could walk down the lane to the old Church. So, after Sunday School, the children used to straggle down to Church without anyone to look after them, and sit on the benches in the aisle and do pretty much what they pleased, except when admonished by Master Oxford's stick.

Mr. Shuckburgh had by this time come to reside in the parish, in the house which is now the post-office, and there was at last a double Service on the Sunday.

The next thing was to consider what was to be done about the boys, who could not be made to mind Mrs. Creswick. A row of the biggest sat at the back of the school, with their heels to the wall, and by constant kicking had almost knocked a hole through the mud wall; so the Vicar, who was now the Archdeacon's son, the Rev. Gilbert Wall Heathcote, gave permission for the putting up another mud and rough cast school house near the old Church, for the boys, in an empty part of the Churchyard to the north-east, where no one had ever been buried.

However, there Master Oxford was installed as schoolmaster, coming all the way down from his house on the hill (a pretty-timbered cottage, now pulled down). He and his boys had a long way to walk to their school, but he taught them all he knew and set them a good example. The boys were all supposed to go to him at six years old, and most were proud of the promotion. One little fellow was known to go to bed an hour or two earlier that he might be six years old the sooner! But some dreaded the good order enforced by the stick. There was one boy in particular, who had outgrown the girls' school, and was very troublesome there. He would not go to the boys', and his mother would not make him, saying she feared he would fall into the water. "Well," said Mrs. Bargus, who was a most bright, kindly old lady of eighty, "I'll make him go." So she took a large piece of yellow glazed calico intended for furniture lining, walked up to school, and held it up to the little boy. She said she heard that he would only go to the girls' school, and, since everybody went there in petticoats, she had brought some stuff to make him a petticoat too! The young man got up and walked straight off to the boys' school.

Here are some verses, written by Mrs. Yonge in 1838, on one of the sights that met her eye in the old Churchyard:—

While on the ear the solemn note
Of prayer and praises heavenward float,
A butterfly with brilliant wings
A lesson full of meaning brings,
        A sermon to the eye.

There on an infant's grave it stands,
For it hath burst the shroud's dull bands,
Its vile worm's body there is left,
Of gross earth's habits now bereft
        It soars into the sky.

Thus when the grave her dead shall give
The little form below shall live,
Clothed in a robe of dazzling white
Shall spring aloft on wings of light,
        To realms above shall fly!

Changes were setting in all this time. The rick-burnings, in which so many foolish persons indulged, was going on in 1831 in many parts of Hampshire. They were caused partly by dislike to the threshing machines that were beginning to be used, and partly by the notion that such disturbances would lead to the passing of the Reform Bill, which ignorant men believed would give every poor man a fat pig in his stye. There was no rick-burning here, though some of the villagers joined the bands of men who wandered about the country demanding money and arms at the large houses. But, happily, none of them were actually engaged in any violence, and none of them swelled the calendar of the Special Assize that took place at Winchester for the trial of the rioters.

One poor maid-servant in the parish, from the North of Hampshire, had, however, two brothers, who were intelligent men of some education, and who, having been ringleaders, were both sentenced to death. The sentence was, however, commuted to transportation for life. At Sydney, being of a very different class from the ordinary convict, they prospered greatly, and their letters were very interesting. They were wonderful feats of penmanship, for postage from Australia was ruinously expensive, and they filled sheets of paper with writing that could hardly be read without a microscope. If we had those letters now they would be curious records of the early days of the

Colony, but all now recollected is the account of a little kangaroo jumping into a hunter's open shirt, thinking it was his mother's pouch.

The Reform Bill, after all, when passed made no present difference in Otterbourne life—nothing like the difference that a measure a few years after effected, namely, the Poor-law Amendment Bill. Not many people here remember the days of the old Poor-law, when whatever a pauper family wanted was supplied from the rates, and thus an idle man often lived more at his ease on other people's money than an industrious man on his own earnings. It was held that if wages were small they might be helped out of the rates, and thus the ratepayers were often ruined. In the midst of the street stood the old Poorhouse. It had no governor nor anyone to see that order was kept or work done there, and everybody that was homeless, or lazy, or disreputable, drifted in there. They went in and out as they pleased, and had a weekly allowance of money. Now and then there was a great row among them. One room was inhabited by an old man named Strong, who was considered a wonder because he ate adders cut up like eels and stewed with a bit of bacon. Every now and then a message would come in that old Strong had got a couple of nice adders and wanted a bit of bacon to cook with them. Then there was a large family whose father never worked for any one long together, and lived in the Workhouse, with a wife and six or seven children, supported by the parish. These people were pursuaded to go to Manchester, where there was sure to be work in the factories for all their many girls. The men in receipt of parish pay were supposed to have work found for them on the roads, but there was not much of this to employ them, and as they were paid all the same whether they worked or not, some were said to hammer the stones as if they were afraid of hurting them, or to make the wheeling a couple of barrows of chalk their whole day's work.

A good deal depended on the vestry management of each parish, and there was less of flagrant idleness supported by the rates here than at many places. There was also a well-built and arranged Workhouse at Hursley, and the Poor law Commissioners consented to make one small Union of Hursley, Otterbourne, Farley, and Baddesley, instead of throwing them into a large one.

The discontinuance of out-door relief to help out the wages was a great shock at first, but, when the ratepayers were no longer weighed down, they could give more work and better wages, and the labourers thus profited in the end, and likewise began to learn more independence. Still the times were hard then. Few families could get on unless the mother as well as the father did field work, and thus she had no time to attend thoroughly to making home comfortable, mending the clothes, or taking care of the little ones. The eldest girl was kept at home dragging about with the baby, and often grew rough as well as ignorant, and the cottage was often very little cared for. The notion of what was comfortable and suitable was very different then.

The country began to be intersected by railways, and the South-Western line was marked out to Southampton. The course was dug out from Shawford and Compton downs, and the embankment made along our valley. It was curious to see the white line creeping on, as carts filled with chalk ran from the diggings to the end, tipped over their contents, and returned again. When the foundations were dug for the arch spanning the lane the holes filled with water as fast as they were made, and nothing could be done till the two long ditches had been dug to carry off the water to Allbrook. In the course of making them in the light peaty earth, some bones of animals and (I believe) stags' horns were found, but unluckily, were thrown away, instead of being shown to anyone who would have made out from them much of the history of the formation of the boggy earth that forms the water meadows.

It is amusing to remember the kind of dread that was felt at first of railway travelling. It was thought that the engines would blow up, and, as an old coachman is reported to have said, "When a coach is overturned, there you are; but when an engine blows up, where are you?" He certainly was so far right that a coach accident was fatal to fewer persons than a railway accident generally is.

The railway passed so near the old Church that the noise of the trains would be inconvenient on Sundays. At least, so thought those with inexperienced ears, though many a Church has since been built much nearer to the line. However, this fixed the purpose that had already been forming, of endeavouring to build a new Church. The first idea had been of trying to raise £300 to enlarge the old Church, but the distance from the greater part of the parish was so inconvenient, and the railroad so near, that the building of a new Church was finally decided on. There really was not room for the men and boys at the same time on the backless forms they occupied between the pews in the chancel. Moreover, if a person was found sitting in a place to which another held that he or she had a right, the owner never thought of looking for another place elsewhere, and the one who was turned out went away displeased, and declared that it was impossible to come to church for fear of "being upset." It is strange and sad that people are so prone to forget what our Master told us about "taking the highest room," even in His own House.

But besides the want of accommodation, the old Church was at an inconvenient distance from the parish. No doubt there had once been more houses near, but when the cottage inhabited by old Aaron Chalk was pulled down, nothing remained near but Otterbourne Farm and the Moat House. Every one living elsewhere had to walk half a mile, some much more, and though Kiln Lane was then much better shaded with fine trees than it is now, it was hard work on a hot or wet Sunday to go twice. Some of us may recollect one constant churchgoer, John Rogers, who was so lame as to require two sticks to walk with, and had to set out an hour beforehand, yet who seldom missed.

Just at this time the Reverend John Keble became Vicar of Hursley, and Otterbourne, and forwarded the plan of church building with all his might.

Few new churches had been built at that time, so that there was everything to be learnt, while subscriptions were being collected from every quarter. Magdalen College, at Oxford, gave the site as well as a handsome subscription, and every endeavour was made to render the new building truly church like. It was during the building that Dr. Rowth, the President of Magdalen College, coming to hold his court at the Moat House, had the model of the church brought out to him and took great interest in it. He is worth remembering, for he was one of the wisest and most learned men in Oxford, and he lived to be nearly a hundred years old. Church building was a much more difficult thing then than it is now, when there are many architects trained in the principles of church building, and materials of all kinds are readily provided.

The cross form was at once fixed on as most suitable; and the little bell turret was copied from one at a place called Corston. Mr. Owen Carter, an architect at Winchester, drew the plans, with the constant watching and direction of Mr. Yonge, who attended to every detail. The white stone, so fit for carving decorations, which had been used in the Cathedral, is imported from Caen, in Normandy. None had been brought over for many years, till a correspondence was opened with the people at the quarries, and blocks bought for the reredos and font. Now it is constantly used.

The panels of the pulpit, with the carvings of the Blessed Virgin, and the four Latin fathers, SS. Ambrose, Augustine, Jerome, and Gregory the Great, were found in a shop for antiquities in London. The shape was adapted to a sounding board, which had been made for the Cathedral, but was rejected there. The altar-rail also was found in a shop. It must previously have been in a church, as it has the sacramental corn and grapes. It is thought to be old Flemish work, and represents a prince on one side with a crown laid down, as he kneels in devotion, and some ladies on the opposite side. The crown is an

Emperor's, and there is the collar of the Golden Fleece round his neck, so that it is probably meant for either the Emperor Maximilian or his grandson, Charles V. One of the gentlemen kneeling behind the Emperor has a beautiful face of adoration.

The building of the Church took about two years, the first stone being laid at the north-east corner. It was begun on the 16th of May, 1837, and it was ready for consecration on the 30th of July, 1839. The building had been prosperous, the only accident being the crushing of a thumb when the pulpit was set in its place.

The new boys' school was built at the same time, the archway of the south door of the old Church being used for the doorway, so as to preserve the beautiful and peculiar decoration, and the roof was lined with the doors and backs of the old oak-pewing. In the flints collected for the building of this and of the wall round the churchyard there was a water wagtail's nest in which a young cuckoo was reared, having, of course, turned out the rightful nestling. Probably it flew safely, for the last time it was seen its foster parents were luring it out with green caterpillars held a little way from the nest.

The expense of the building of the boys' school and of a new room for the girls was defrayed chiefly by a bazaar held at Winchester. There were at that time no Education Acts nor Government requirements, and the buildings would be deemed entirely unfit at this time even for the numbers who then used them, and who did not amount to more than between thirty and forty boys and fifty or sixty girls and infants, together about a third of the present numbers at school in Otterbourne and Allbrook. Miss Tucker was then the mistress; Master Oxford still the master.

The Church was consecrated on the 30th of July, 1839, by Bishop Sumner, who preached a sermon on the text, "No man careth for my soul," warning us that we could not plead such an excuse for ourselves, if we neglected to walk in the right way.

One of the earliest funerals in the churchyard was that of good old Oxford, old, as he was called, because he was crippled by rheumatism, but he was only fifty-two. He lies buried near the south gate of the churchyard under a large slate recording his name.

He was followed in his office by Mr. William Stainer, who had hitherto been known as a baker, living in the house which is now Mr. James Godwin's. His bread was excellent, and he was also noted for what were called Otterbourne buns, the art of making which seems to have gone with him. They were small fair-complexioned buns, which stuck together in parties of three, and when soaked, expanded to twice or three times their former size. He used to send them once or twice a week to Winchester. But though baking was his profession, he did much besides. He was a real old-fashioned herbalist, and had a curious book on the virtues of plants, and he made decoctions of many kinds, which he administered to those in want of medicine. Before the Poor Law provided Union doctors, medical advice, except at the hospital, was almost out of reach of the poor. Mr. and Mrs. Yonge, like almost all other beneficent gentlefolks in villages, kept a medicine chest and book, and doctored such cases as they could venture on, and Mr. Stainer was in great favour as practitioner, as many of our elder people can remember. He was exceedingly charitable and kind, and ready to give his help so far as he could. He was a great lover of flowers, and had contrived a sort of little greenhouse over the great oven at the back of his house, and there he used to bring up lovely geraniums and other flowers, which he sometimes sold. He was a deeply religious and devout man, and during Master Oxford's illness took his place in Church, which was more important when there was no choir and the singers sat in the gallery. He was very happy in this office, moving about on felt shoes that he might make no noise, and most reverently keeping the Church clean and watching over it in every way. He also continued in the post of schoolmaster, which at first he had only taken temporarily, giving up part of his business to his nephew. But he still sat up at night baking, and he also had other troubles: there was insanity in his family, and he was much harassed.

His kindness and simplicity were sometimes abused. He never had the heart to refuse to lend money, or to deny bread on credit to hopeless debtors; and altogether debts, distress, baking all night, and school keeping all day, were too much for him. The first hint of an examination of his school completed the mischief, and he died insane. It is a sad story, but many of us will remember with affectionate regard the good, kind, quaint, and most excellent little man. By that time our schoolmistress was Mrs. Durndell, the policeman's wife, a severe woman, but she certainly made the girls do thoroughly whatever she taught, especially repetition and needlework.

The examiner on religious subjects, Mr. Allen, afterwards an Archdeacon, reported that the girls had an unusual knowledge of the text of Scripture, but that he did not think them equally intelligent as to the meaning.

Daily Service had been commenced when the new Church was opened, and the children of the schools attended it. There was also a much larger congregation of old men than have ever come in later years. At one time there were nine constantly there. One of these, named Passingham, who used to ring the bell for matins and evensong, was said to have been the strongest man in the parish, and to have carried two sacks of corn over the common on the top of the hill in his youth. He was still a hearty old man at eighty-six, when after ringing the bell one morning as usual, he dropped down on the hill in a fit and died in a few seconds.

There was not much change for a good many years. In 1846, the Parsonage House was built and given to the living by Mr. Keble. The stained glass of the south window of the Church was given by the Reverend John Yonge, of Puslinch, Rector of Newton Ferrers, in Devonshire, in memory of his youngest son, Edmund Charles, who died at Otterbourne House in 1847. Thirteen years previously, in 1834, the eldest son, James Yonge, had likewise died at Otterbourne House. Both the brothers lie buried here, one in the old churchyard, one in the new. They are commemorated in their own church at Newton by a tablet with the inscription—"What I do thou knowest not now, but thou shall know hereafter."

In 1834 their father gave what made, as it were the second foundation of the Lending Library, for there were about four-and-twenty very serious books, given in Archdeacon Heathcote's time, kept in the vestry at the old Church. They looked as if they had been read but only by the elder people who liked a grave book, and there was nothing there meant for the young people. So there were a good many new books bought, and weekly given out at the Penny Club, with more or less vigour, for the next thirty years or so.

The next public matter that greatly affected this place was the Crimean War. It was a large proportion of our young men who were more or less concerned in it. Captain Denzill Chamberlayne in the Cavalry, Lieut. Julian B. Yonge, John Hawkins, Joseph Knight, James and William Mason, and it was in the midst of the hurry and confusion of the departure that the death of Mr. W. C. Yonge took place, February 26th, 1854. Three of those above mentioned lived to return home. Captain Chamberlayne shared in the famous charge of the Light Brigade, at Balaclava, when

> Into the jaws of death
> Rode the six hundred:
> Cannon to right of them,
> Cannon to left of them,
> Volleyed and thundered.

His horse, Pimento, was killed under him, but he escaped without a wound, and on his return home was drawn up to the house by the people, and had a reception which made such an impression on the children that when one was asked in school what a hero was, she answered, "Captain Chamberlayne."

John Hawkins, Joseph Knight, and William Mason died in the Crimea. A tablet to commemorate them was built into the wall of the churchyard, with the text—"It is good for a man that he bear the yoke in his youth," for the discipline of the army had been very good for these youths, and, therefore, this verse was chosen for them by Mr. Keble.

The next event that concerned the parish much was the death of the great and holy man who had been our rector for thirty years. Mr. Keble died at Bournemouth on the 29th of March, 1866. His manners and language were always so simple, and his humility so great, that many of those who came in contact with him never realized how great a man he was, not being able to perceive that the very deepest thoughts might be clothed in the plainest language. Some felt, in the words of the poem,—

"I came and saw, and having seen,
  Weak heart! I drew offence
From thy prompt smile, thy humble mien,
  Thy lowly diligence."

But none who really knew him could fail to be impressed with the sense of his power, his wisdom, his love, and, above all, his holiness; and his *Christian Year* will always be a fund of consolation, full of suggestions of good and devotional thoughts and deeds. Mrs. Keble, who was already very ill, followed him to her rest on the 11th of May. It may be worth remembering that the last time she wrote her name was a signature to a petition against licensing marriage with a deceased wife's sister.

Sir William Heathcote then appointed the Reverend James G. Young as Vicar of Hursley and Otterbourne. A fresh tide of change began to set in. As times altered and population increased, and as old things and people passed away, there were various changes in the face of the village. The Government requirements made it necessary to erect a new Girl's School, and land was permanently secured for the purpose, and this was done chiefly by subscription among the inhabitants, affording a room large enough for parish meetings and lectures, as well as for its direct purpose. The subscription was as a testimonial to the Rev. William Bigg-Wither, who had been thirty years curate of the parish, and under whom many of the changes for the better were worked out. The building was provided with a tower, in case there should ever be a clock given to the parish.

The clock was given in a manner worthy of remembrance. Mr. William Pink, as a thatcher, and his two sisters in service, had saved enough to provide for their old age, and to leave a considerable overplus, out of which the last survivor, Mrs. Elizabeth Pink, when passing away at a good old age, bequeathed enough to provide the parish with the clock whose voice has already become one of our most familiar sounds.

Allbrook was by this time growing into a large hamlet, and a school chapel was then built, chiefly by Mr. Wheeler. We must not forget that we had for five years the great and excellent Samuel Wilberforce for our Bishop, and that he twice held confirmations in our parish. No one can forget the shock of his sudden call. One moment he was calling his companion's attention to the notes of a late singing nightingale; the next, his horse had stumbled and he was gone. It was remarkable that shortly before he had, after going over the hospital, spoken with dread of what he called the "humiliation of a lingering illness"—exactly what he was spared.

Bishop Harold Browne came from Ely to take the See of Winchester. He reconsecrated our church when the chancel was enlarged and the new aisle added. He carried on vigorously work only begun under Bishop Wilberforce. Under him Diocesan Synods, the Girls' Friendly Society, and the Examination of Senior Scholars in Religious Knowledge have all shown his diligent oversight as Shepherd of the flock.

In the year 1875 Sir William Heathcote succeeded in bringing about an arrangement by which Otterbourne could be separated from Hursley and have a Vicar of its own, the difference of income being made up to the Vicar of Hursley. This was done by the aid of a munificent lady, Mrs. Gibbs, the widow of one of the great merchant princes, whose wealth was always treated as a trust from God. She became the patron of the living, and the advowson remains in her family.

The first Vicar was the Reverend Walter Francis Elgie, who had already been six years curate, and had won the love and honour of all his flock. Deeply did they all mourn him when it was God's will to take him from them on the 25th of February, 1881, in the 43rd year of his age, after ten years of zealous work.

It was felt as remarkable that a young pupil teacher in consumption, whom he had sent to the Home at Bournemouth, was taken on the same day, and buried here the day after, and that the schoolmaster, Walter Fisher, a man of gentle and saintly nature, followed him six weeks after.

We left them in the Church's shade,
  Our standard-bearer true,
And near at hand the gentle maid
  Who well his guidance knew.

He fainted in the noon of life,
  Nor knew his victory won;
She was fresh girded for the strife,

Her battle scarce begun.

Long had we known Death's angel hand
The maiden's brow had seal'd;
He fell, like chief of warrior band,
Struck down on battle-field.

So in God's acre here they meet
As they have met above,
Tasting beneath their Saviour's feet
The treasures of His love.

For what they learnt and taught of here
Is present with them there;
May we speed on in faith and fear,
Then heavenly rest to share.

With the coming of our present Vicar, the Rev. H. W. Brock, our Otterbourne story ends, as the times are no longer *old times*. The water works for the supply of Southampton are our last novelty, by which such of us benefit, as either themselves or their landlords pay a small contribution. They have given us some red buildings at one end and on the Hill a queer little round tower containing the staircase leading to the underground reservoir, a wonderful construction of circles of brick pillars and arches, as those remember who visited it before the water was let in. And, verily, we may be thankful that our record has so few events in it, no terrible disasters, but that there has been peace and health and comfort, more than falls to the lot of many a parish. Truly we may thankfully say, "The lot is fallen unto me in a fair ground, yea, I have a goodly heritage."

Old Remembrances.

I remember, I remember,
  Old times at Otterbourne,
Before the building of the Church,
  And when smock frocks were worn!

I remember, I remember,
  When railroads there were none,
When by stage coach at early dawn
  The journey was begun.

And through the turnpike roads till eve
  Trotted the horses four,
With inside passengers and out
  They carried near a score.

"Red Rover" and the "Telegraph,"
  We knew them all by name,
And Mason's and the Oxford coach,
  Full thirty of them came.

The coachman wore his many capes,
  The guard his bugle blew;
The horses were a gallant sight,
  Dashing upon our view.

I remember, I remember,
  The posting days of old;
The yellow chariot lined with blue
  And lace of colour gold.

The post-boys' jackets blue or buff,
  The inns upon the road;
The hills up which we used to walk
  To lighten thus the load.

The rattling up before the inn,
  The horses led away,

The post-boy as he touched his hat
  And came to ask his pay.

The perch aloft upon the box,
  Delightful for the view;
The turnpike gates whose keepers stood
  Demanding each his due.

I remember, I remember,
  When ships were beauteous things,
The floating castles of the deep
  Borne upon snow-white wings;

Ere iron-clads and turret ships,
  Ugly as evil dream,
Became the hideous progeny
  Of iron and of steam.

You crossed the Itchen ferry
  All in an open boat,
Now, on a panting hissing bridge
  You scarcely seem afloat.

Southampton docks were sheets of mud,
  Grim colliers at the quay.
No tramway, and no slender pier
  To stretch into the sea.

I remember, I remember,
  Long years ere Rowland Hill,
When letters covered quarto sheets
  Writ with a grey goose quill;

Both hard to fold and hard to read,
  Crossed to the scarlet seal;
Hardest of all to pay for ere
  Their news they might reveal.

No stamp with royal head was there,
  But eightpence was the sum
For every letter, all alike,
  That did from London come!

I remember, I remember,
  The mowing of the hay;
Scythes sweeping through the heavy grass
  At breaking of the day.

The haymakers in merry ranks
  Tossing the swaths so sweet,
The haycocks tanning olive-brown
  In glowing summer heat.

The reapers 'mid the ruddy wheat,
  The thumping of the flail,
The winnowing within the barn
  By whirling round a sail.

Long ere the whirr, and buz, and rush
  Became a harvest sound,
Or monsters trailed their tails of spikes,
  Or ploughed the fallow ground.

Our sparks flew from the flint and steel,
  No lucifers were known,
Snuffers with tallow candles came
  To prune the wick o'ergrown.

Hands did the work of engines then,
  But now some new machine
Must hatch the eggs, and sew the seams,
  And make the cakes, I ween.

I remember, I remember,
  The homely village school,
The dame with spelling book and rod,
  The sceptre of her rule.

A black silk bonnet on her head,
  Buff kerchief on her neck,
With spectacles upon her nose,
  And apron of blue check.

Ah, then were no inspection days,
  No standards then were known,
Children could freely make dirt pies,
  And learning let alone!

Those Sundays I remember too,
  When Service there was one;
For living in the parish then
  Of clergy there were none.

And oh, I can recall to mind,
  The Church and every pew;

William and Mary's royal arms
  Hung up in fullest view.

The lion smiling, with his tongue
  Like a pug dog's hung out;
The unicorn with twisted horn
  Brooding upon his rout.

Exalted in the gallery high
  The tuneful village choir,
With flute, bassoon, and clarionet,
  Their notes rose high and higher.

They shewed the number of the Psalm
  In white upon a slate,
And many a time the last lines sung
  Of Brady and of Tate.

While far below upon the floor
  Along the narrow aisle,
The children on then benches sat
  Arranged in single file

And there the clerk would stump along
  And strike with echoing blow
Each idle guilty little head
  That chattered loud or low.

Ah! I remember many things,
  Old middle-aged, and new;
Is the new better than the old,
  More bright, more wise, more true?

The old must ever pass away,
  The new must still come in;
When these new things are old to you
  Be they unstained by sin.

So will their memory be sweet,
  A treasury of bliss
To be borne with us in the days
  When we their presence miss.

Trifles connected with the love
  Of many a vanished friend
Will thrill the heart and wake the sense,
  For memory has no end!

www.ingramcontent.com/pod-product-compliance
Lightning Source LLC
Chambersburg PA
CBHW060800310726
48980CB00002B/169
* 9 7 8 3 7 3 2 6 1 9 3 7 5 *